A Michael Neugebauer Book

NORTH-SOUTH BOOKS / NEW YORK / LONDON

HANS CHRISTIAN ANDERSEN
LISBETH ZWERGER

THE SWINEHERD

TRANSLATED FROM THE DANISH BY ANTHEA BELL

Once upon a time there was a prince, and he was poor. He had a kingdom: only a little one, but still, it was big enough for him to marry on the strength of it, and he wanted to get married. He was really aiming rather high in daring to ask the emperor's daughter, "Will you have me?" All the same, that is what he did, since his name was known far and wide, and there were hundreds of princesses who would have said yes. But what did the emperor's daughter say? Well, we shall see!

There was a rose tree growing on the grave of the prince's father, and what a beautiful rose tree it was. It flowered only once in five years, and then it bore only one rose, but that rose had so sweet a fragrance that anyone who smelled it forgot all his cares and sorrows. And the prince also had a nightingale that could sing as if its little throat held all the lovely music in the world. He thought he would give the rose and the nightingale to the princess, so they were put into large silver caskets and sent to her.

The emperor had the caskets brought before him in the great hall, where the princess and her ladies-in-waiting were playing "Going Visiting." That was all they ever did with their time. When the princess saw the big caskets holding her presents, she clapped her hands for joy.

"I hope there's a little cat inside!" she said. However, what they found was the lovely rose.

"Isn't it nicely made!" said the ladies-in-waiting.

"Nicely?" said the emperor. "It's better than nice, it is beautiful!"

But when the princess touched the rose, she could have wept.

"Oh dear, Papa!" said she. "It isn't artificial after all, it's REAL!"

"Oh dear!" said all the courtiers. "It's real!"

"Well, let's see what's in the other casket before we lose our tempers," said the emperor. Out came the nightingale. It sang so sweetly that at first they could not say a word against it.

"SUPERBE! CHARMANT!" remarked the ladies-in-waiting, who all spoke French, and spoke it very badly.

"That bird reminds me of the late empress's musical box!" said one old courtier. "The notes and the way it sings are just the same."

"So they are," said the emperor, and he wept like a little child.

"You can't tell me THAT'S real!" said the princess.

"Oh yes, it's a real bird sure enough," said the man who had brought it.

"Then it can fly away!" said the princess, and nothing would persuade her to let the prince come and see her.

But he was not going to lose heart; he smeared his face with dirt, leaving black and brown marks, jammed his hat down on his head, and knocked on the emperor's door.

"Good day, emperor!" said he. "Can I have a job at the palace?"

"Dear me, there are so many people who want to work here!" said the emperor. "However, let's see – I do need someone to look after the pigs; we have a great many pigs."

So the prince was made court swineherd. He was given a miserable little room near the pigsty, and there he had to stay. He sat and worked all day, and by the time evening came he had made a nice little pan with bells all around it. As soon as the pan came to the boil, the bells rang out very prettily, playing the old tune:

"OH, MY DEAREST AUGUSTINE,
ALL'S LOST, LOST, LOST!"

However, the most remarkable thing of all was that when you held your finger in the steam coming from the pan, you would immediately smell what was being cooked on every hearth in town. That was certainly a far cry from the rose!

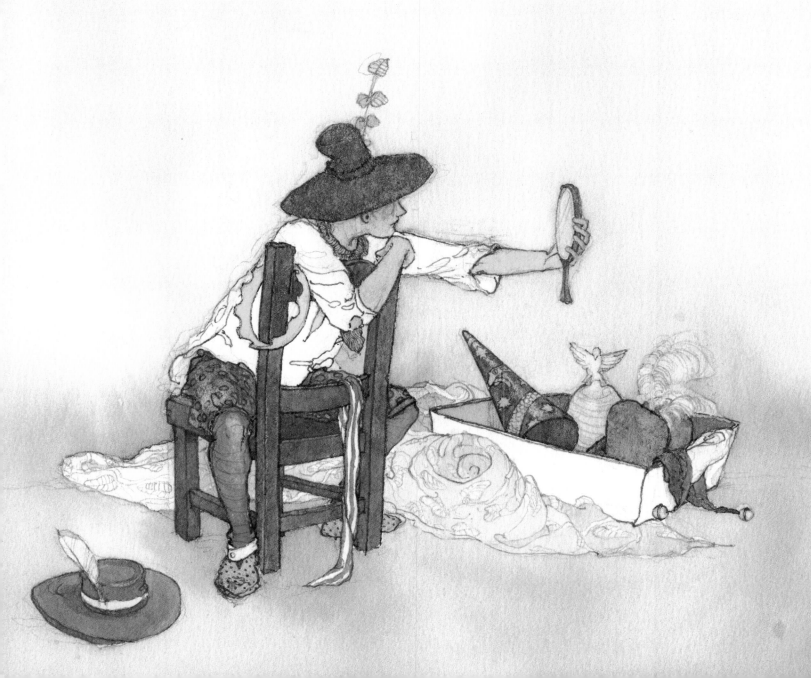

Along came the princess with all her ladies-in-waiting, and she heard the tune. She stopped and looked pleased; the fact was, she could play "Oh, my dearest Augustine" herself. Indeed, it was the ONLY tune she could play, and she played it with one finger at that.

"That's my own tune!" she said. "What a well-educated swineherd he must be!

Go in and ask him what his musical instrument costs."

So one of the ladies-in-waiting went in, putting wooden clogs on first.

"What do you want for that pan?" asked the lady-in-waiting.

"Ten kisses from the princess," said the swineherd.

"Mercy on us!" said the lady.

"I can't take less." said the swineherd.

"Well," asked the princess, "what did he say?"

"Oh dear," said the lady-in-waiting, "I really can't bring myself to tell you, it's so shocking!"

"Then whisper it!" So the lady whispered.

"Good gracious, how rude of him!" said the princess, and she walked away.

But she had not gone far before the bells rang out with their pretty tune again:

"OH, MY DEAREST AUGUSTINE,
ALL'S LOST, LOST, LOST!"

"Go and ask him if he'll take ten kisses from my ladies instead," said the princess.

"No, thank you," said the swineherd. "Ten kisses from the princess, or I keep my pan."

"The impertinence of it!" said the princess. "Oh, well, you must all stand in front of me so nobody can see."

So the ladies-in-waiting stood in front of her and held out the skirts of their dresses, and the swineherd got his ten kisses, and the princess got the pan.

What fun the princess and her ladies had! They made the pan boil all evening, and all next day, and they knew what was cooking on every fire in town, from the lord chamberlain's hearth to the cobbler's. The ladies-in-waiting danced about, clapping their hands. "We know who's having sweet soup and who's having pancakes! We know who's having porridge and who's having cutlets! Isn't that interesting?"

"Very interesting indeed," said the mistress of the royal household.

"But you must keep it secret," said the princess, because I'm the emperor's daughter!"

"Of course we will," everyone said.

The swineherd, who was really the prince – though they didn't know it and thought he was a real swineherd – did not sit idle all day. He made a rattle. When you swung the rattle around, it played all the waltzes and jigs and polkas that have ever been heard since the world began.

"How delightful!" said the princess as she walked by. "I never heard a better tune! Go in and ask him what that instrument costs – mind you I'm not kissing him again!"

"He wants a hundred kisses from the princess," said the lady who had gone to ask.

"He must be crazy!" said the princess, and she walked away, but before she had gone far she stopped. "Well, one must encourage Art," said she, "and I AM the emperor's daughter! Tell him I'll give him ten kisses, the same as yesterday, and he can have the rest from my ladies."

"Oh," said the ladies, "we wouldn't like that."

"Nonsense!" said the princess. "If I can kiss him, so can you. Don't forget I pay your wages!"

So the lady–in–waiting had to go and see the swineherd again.

"A hundred kisses from the princess herself," he said, "or we each keep what's our own."

"Stand in front of me," said the princess, so all the ladies-in-waiting stood in front of her, and the swineherd started kissing.

"What's that crowd doing down by the pigsty?" asked the emperor, who had gone out onto his balcony, and he rubbed his eyes and put his spectacles on.

"Oh, it's the ladies-in-waiting playing some kind of game. I'll go and see what they're up to!" And he pulled on his slippers, which were trodden down at the heel.

He was in a great hurry!

As soon as he was down in the courtyard, he went along very quietly. The ladies–in–waiting were so busy counting kisses, to make sure it was all fair and the swineherd did not get too many or too few, that they never noticed the emperor. He stood on tiptoe.

"What's all this?" said he, seeing the kissing, and he hit them over the head with his slipper just as the swineherd was taking his eighty–sixth kiss.

"Get out!" said the emperor, really furious, and the princess and the swineherd were both turned out of his empire.

So there stood the princess, crying, and the swineherd was angry, and the rain poured down.

"Poor me! I'm so miserable!" said the princess. "If only I'd taken that handsome prince! Oh, how unhappy I am!"

Then the swineherd went behind a tree, wiped the black and brown smears off his face, cast his dirty clothes aside and came back in his royal robes, looking so fine that the princess bowed down to him.

"Now that I know you, I despise you!" he said. "You wouldn't marry an honest prince, you didn't know the true value of the rose and the nightingale, but you were ready to kiss the swineherd just for a toy! It serves you right."

And he went home to his own kingdom and shut and locked the door. All she could do was stand outside and sing:

"OH, MY DEAREST AUGUSTINE,
ALL'S LOST, LOST, LOST!"

First North-South Books edition published in 1995.
Copyright © 1982 by Michael Neugebauer Verlag AG, Gossau Zurich, Switzerland
First published in German under the title DER SCHWEINEHIRT
English translation is used with the kind permission of William Morrow & Company, New York.

Distributed in the United States by North-South Books Inc., New York

Library of Congress Cataloging-in-Publication Data
Andersen, H.C. (Hans Christian), 1805-1875.
The Swineherd.
Translation of: Svinedrengen.
Summary: A prince disguises himself as a swineherd and learns the
true character of the princess he desires.
[1. Fairy tales]   I. Zwerger, Lisbeth, ill.   II. Bell, Anthea.   III. Title
PZ8.A542Sw. 1982 [E] 81-14173
ISBN 1-55858-428-5 (trade edition)
ISBN 1-55858-429-3 (paperback)

British Library Cataloguing in Publication Data is available

TR 10 9 8 7 6 5 4 3 2 1
PB 10 9 8 7 6 5 4 3 2 1
Printed in Italy